PARENTS' MAGAZINE PRESS, INC.
52 Vanderbilt Ave., New York 17, N. Y.

AN ELEPHANT IS NOT A CAT

by Alvin Tresselt and Wilbur Wheaton • illustrated by Tom Vroman

PIETER VANDERLOON was a very fortunate man. He had a fine fat wife. He had six roly-poly children. And he had the best mill in all of Holland.

Everyone agreed that Pieter's mill ground corn better than any other mill in the land. From miles around people came to buy ground corn from Pieter. And from miles around people brought their corn to be ground into meal.

Some brought sacks of corn on their backs. Some brought sacks of corn in creaky wheelbarrows. And others rode up in horse-drawn wagons because they had so many sacks of corn for Pieter to grind.

Now, since he charged three pieces of
silver for each sack, Pieter grew richer
every day. His fine fat wife grew jollier,
and his six roly-poly children bloomed like
roses.

But one sunny morning, Pieter went into his mill to start the grinding wheels, and what did he see? Two tiny mice, as bold as brass, sitting on a sack and having a fine breakfast of four kernels of corn.

Well, Pieter Vanderloon was very upset! "Wife! Wife!" he cried, running into the house. "We are poorer today than we were yesterday, and we'll be even poorer tomorrow!"

"Why, how can that be?" asked his wife with a laugh. "Everyone knows our mill grinds more corn than any other mill in all of Holland!"

"True, true," replied Pieter. "But just now, when I went into the mill to start the grinding, I saw two mice. And right before my very eyes they ate four grains of corn!"

At this, his jolly wife laughed so hard she had to wipe the tears from her eyes with the corner of her apron. "And how can four kernels of corn make us richer or poorer?" she asked, when she had caught her breath.

"Laugh if you will," said Pieter. "But if they took four today, they'll take more tomorrow, and each day we will indeed grow poorer."

Now, Pieter's wife was a kind-hearted soul, and very thankful for all their blessings. "Surely we have more than enough," she said. "Let the mice have their bit to eat. Who knows—one day they may even repay your kindness."

But Pieter continued to fuss and fume, till at last his wife suggested that he go into the village and buy a cat. "A fine mouser will put an end to your worries," she said. "And then perhaps you can get back to work again."

"An excellent idea!" exclaimed Pieter. "How blessed I am to have such a clever wife!" And he set out at once down the road to the village.

He hadn't gone very far when he came upon a strange-looking man, sitting at the side of the road. And stranger still, he

was surrounded by a collection of wagons
and cages, draped with tattered flags and
banners.

"Ah, how do you do, my friend," said the stranger, bowing low. "And what brings you out on this dusty road on such a lovely day? Perhaps you would care to

stop for a moment, sit in the shade of my noble caravan and listen while I tell a tale or two."

"Thank you kindly," replied Pieter, "but I must hurry into the village to buy a cat."

"A cat!" exclaimed the man. "Ah, yes. A fine animal. But why settle for such an ordinary beast? Let me sell you a pair of

guinea hens

or a waltzing gazelle,

a panda from the Punjab

or a black panther from darkest Africa!"

"No," said Pieter. "All I want is a cat to guard my mill."

"A cat, indeed!" said the strange man, looking down his long nose. "You don't want a cat; you want an elephant. For it

is perfectly clear to anyone with eyes that from the tip of his trunk to the end of his tail, there is far more to an elephant than there is to a cat!"

And with that, the man drew aside a curtain.

Poor Pieter could only stand and gape, with his jaw hanging down to his chest, for there in front of him stood a great gray elephant. "Indeed that is true," he said, when he had overcome his astonishment.

And he thought to himself, "Such a big animal would guard my mill from thieves as well as mice!"

Without wasting a moment he reached for his bag of coins and asked how much the elephant would cost.

"Wel-l-l," said the stranger, with a sly smile, "let me see." And he began counting —first all his fingers, then his two ears and his nose. "Hmmm," he said. Then he sat down, took off his shoes and began adding up his ten toes.

"Hurry up!" cried Pieter impatiently. "I have work to do, and the morning is half over already!"

The stranger stopped his counting and said crossly, "Now look what you've done! You made me lose count, just as I got to my middle-size toe." Then, quickly, he broke into a broad smile. "But since you are a busy man with little time to waste, you may have the elephant with my compliments, *if*"—and he paused for a moment, "you promise never to bring him back again."

"For nothing!" cried Pieter, scarcely believing his ears, and without bothering to find out why the stranger was willing to give away such a noble animal, he scrambled up onto the back of the elephant and started down the road lest the man change his mind.

"Thank you, thank you," cried Pieter, for he did remember his manners, and off he went in a cloud of yellow dust.

"Just remember to feed him lots of corn," called the stranger, but the miller was too far down the road to hear a word.

The nearer Pieter got to his mill, the happier he became. Never had a day seemed so fair. Never had the air felt so fresh. Never had he had such a fine view of the broad fields of Holland as he did

from the top of his elephant's back. And he laughed to think how the mice would scoot and scamper when they saw an elephant guarding the corn!

And so in a short time he arrived back at his house. But when his jolly wife saw the good miller Pieter Vanderloon riding up on the back of an elephant, she thought for a minute that she had lost her senses!

"Good wife," Pieter said to her, "look what I have to guard our corn! And I didn't have to pay a single gold coin for him!"

With a shriek his wife fled into the house and bolted the door. "You should have bought a cat!" she cried through the keyhole. "Not an elephant!"

"That shows how foolish you are," said
Pieter. "For why should I pay for a cat,
when I can get an elephant for nothing?

Besides, anyone can see that from the tip of his trunk to the end of his tail, there is far more to an elephant than there is to a cat!" And with that, Pieter slid down from the elephant's back and led him into the mill.

But then the trouble began. The elephant
no sooner got through the door of the mill
when his eyes fell on the corn—sacks and

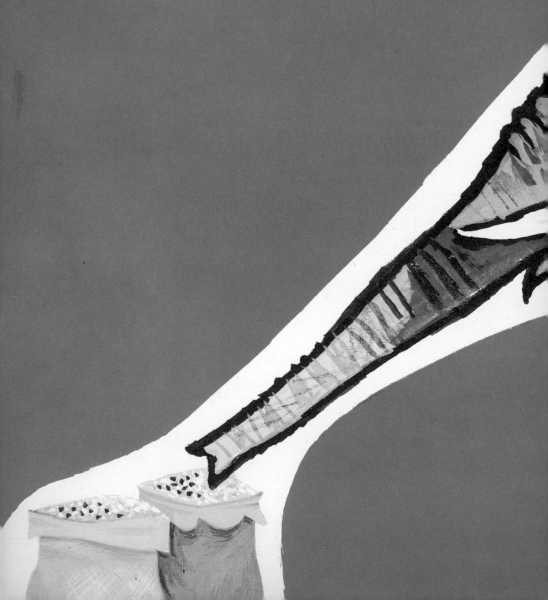

sacks of yellow corn! With a squeal of joy,
a swish of his trunk and a *crunch crunch
crunch*, he started to gobble up the nearest
sack.

"No, no!" cried Pieter. "You're supposed to guard my corn, not eat it!"

But the elephant paid him no mind. Having finished off the first sack, he lumbered over to the next, and with a swish of his trunk and a *crunch crunch crunch* he went right on eating.

The poor miller was beside himself. He waved his hands. He yelled. He pulled on the elephant's tail and jumped up and down. But to no avail. The elephant went right on eating—two sacks, three sacks, a fourth and a fifth.

Pieter sank down in a heap and buried his head in his hands. "Now I know," he moaned. "Now I know why the strange man was so willing to give away his elephant. Why didn't I listen to my good wife and buy a cat?"

Now, the two mice who had started all this trouble were still hiding in the crack in the wall. Hearing all the commotion, and being more curious than timid, they scampered out to see what was going on.

And then a most amazing thing happened. The great gray elephant took one look at the tiny scurrying mice and flattened back his ears. Raising his trunk, he trumpeted for all he was worth, blowing out a few last kernels of corn as he did so. Then, with his trunk held high and his tail tucked in, he bolted for the door.

Back down the road he ran in a cloud
of yellow dust, just as fast as his four fat
legs would take him. Back to his master, the

circus man. And that's how Pieter found
out what everybody knows—elephants are
frightened to death of mice!

Meanwhile, Pieter's good wife had been keeping an eye on what was going on, and as soon as she saw the elephant run off, she ventured out of the house and into the mill. There sat her husband in a heap on the floor, and the two mice on a sack of corn, squeaking busily together about the silly thing that had just happened.

"There, there," she said, with a jolly laugh. "We still have a few sacks of corn left, and if you just get back to work, we'll soon be richer than we were before."

And so it was. Pieter's mill went right on grinding corn better than any other mill in Holland. People still brought corn to him to grind, on their backs, in wheelbarrows and wagons. And three jingly pieces of silver for each sack soon made Pieter a rich man again.

What about the two tiny mice? Well, they went right on living in the mill, eating corn to their hearts' content. And Pieter and his jolly fat wife and six roly-poly children were delighted to have them there — just in case that elephant should ever decide to come around for another meal.

As for the stranger, he's still trying to trick someone into taking—and keeping—his huge hungry elephant.